ISSUES THAT CONCERN YOU

Peer Pressure

Other books in the Issues That Concern You series:

Activism
Alternate Energy
Disaster Relief
Divorce and Children
English Language Learners
Going Green
Mental Illness
Money Management
Prejudice
Recycling
School Violence
Teen Pregnancy
Teen Suicide

ISSUES THAT CONCERN YOU

Peer Pressure

Lorraine Savage, *Book Editor*

GREENHAVEN PRESS
A part of Gale, Cengage Learning

GALE
CENGAGE Learning™

Detroit • New York • San Francisco • New Haven, Conn • Waterville, Maine • London

GALE
CENGAGE Learning™

Christine Nasso, *Publisher*
Elizabeth Des Chenes, *Managing Editor*

Articles in Greenhaven Press anthologies are often edited for length to meet page require-ments. In addition, original titles of these works are changed to clearly present the main thesis and to explicitly indicate the author's opinion. Every effort is made to ensure that Greenhaven Press accurately reflects the original intent of the authors. Every effort has been made to trace the owners of copyrighted material.

Cover image copyright Timothy Large, 2009. Used under license from Shutterstock.com.

LIBRARY OF CONGRESS CATALOGING-IN-PUBLICATION DATA

Peer pressure / Lorraine Savage, book editor.
  p. cm. -- (Issues that concern you)
 Includes bibliographical references and index.
 ISBN 978-0-7377-3987-9 (hbk.)
 1. Peer pressure in adolescence--Juvenile literature. 2. Peer pressure--Juvenile litera-ture. I. Savage, Lorraine.
 HQ799.2.P44P44 2009
 303.3'2709835--dc22

                                                                    2008052823

Printed in the United States of America
1 2 3 4 5 6 7 13 12 11 10 09

CONTENTS

INTRODUCTION

Peer pressure affects most children and adolescents. It is inevitable that kids will experience peer pressure in school, in sports activities, at camp, at parties, and wherever they hang out. Many kids want to do the right thing, follow the rules, be good students, and not get into dangerous activities. But the lure of peer pressure is ever present.

Peer pressure makes kids want to do what the "cool" kids are doing, to fit in, to be popular, to share the experiences of other kids. Sometimes this peer pressure is harmless, like wanting to listen to the same music, wear the same fashions, or have the same haircut. But peer pressure can also lead to harmful or illegal activities, such as smoking, drinking, having sex, fighting, shoplifting, and engaging in risky or daredevil antics.

The reasons for the appeal of peer pressure are varied. Recent research into the brain activity of adolescents reveals that the brains of twelve- to twenty-year-olds are still developing and do not yet have the reasoning ability and impulse control of adults. Adolescents are not able to project into the future to understand the possible consequences of the risks they take right now. Instead, they are hardwired toward impulsive behavior. To them, it is more important to follow the crowd, no matter the results of their actions.

Some studies have shown that susceptibility to peer pressure tapers off in later adolescence and early adulthood and that self-esteem and a desire to make one's own choices in life take precedence. This is true for many people who grow up and move into the adult world of jobs, careers, and family. They replace high school or college friends with business colleagues and associates, teammates, and neighborhood friends.

Even if adolescents are more prone to peer pressure, adults are not immune to it. The urge to follow the crowd, not stand out,

Peer pressure can lead to harmful activities such as smoking, drinking, and risky behavior.

and do what your neighbors or colleagues are doing remains strong in most adults. It is often called "keeping up with the Joneses." This can be beneficial, such as wanting to follow your neighbors in conserving electricity, recycling in your community, or even losing weight. It can also be harmful, as when rowdy men or drunken sports fans gather together to commit violence or vandalism.

Positive and Negative Peer Pressure

Peer pressure can steer young people right as well as wrong. Studies have shown that peer pressure from best friends is a major factor in avoiding harmful peer pressure. If best friends do not smoke, drink, take drugs, or engage in sex, or if they actively disapprove of these actions, then friends in their peer group are more apt to avoid these behaviors.

Positive peer influence can promote good values, unify kids, encourage teamwork, promote respect for adults and other kids, persuade kids not to lie or exaggerate to get out of situations, and encourage kids to take responsibility for what they do. In specific instances, if a child gets good grades or loses weight or joins a sports team, others in his group are likely to follow. In the best of worlds, positive peer pressure can be used to influence bullies in the schoolyard into acting better toward other kids and giving up their aggressive tactics.

Parents too influence adolescents for good or bad. Studies have shown that children are more likely to smoke or drink if their parents smoke or drink. If teens know their parents would disapprove of these behaviors, they are less likely to engage in

Positive peer pressure can promote good values and encourage teamwork and personal responsibility.

risky or unlawful activities. These disapproving parents are more likely to talk with their kids about the harmful effects of drugs, alcohol, and smoking.

In *Issues That Concern You: Peer Pressure*, experts and others weigh in on peer pressure's causes, effects, and consequences. In addition, the volume includes a bibliography, a list of organizations to contact for further information, and other useful appendixes. The appendix titled "What You Should Know About Peer Pressure" offers vital facts about the subject and how it affects young people. The appendix "What You Should Do About Peer Pressure" discusses various solutions to the problem of peer pressure. These many useful features make *Issues That Concern You: Peer Pressure* a valuable resource. Given the growing social and financial costs of peer pressure to society, having a greater understanding of this issue is critical.

ONE

Peer Pressure:
An Overview

Maria R.T. de Guzman

> Maria R.T. de Guzman is the adolescent development exten-
> sion specialist and assistant professor of family and consumer
> sciences in the Department of Psychology, University of
> Nebraska–Lincoln. She writes about adolescent and youth
> issues. In the following viewpoint de Guzman reports that peer
> pressure and peer influence is inevitable during adolescents'
> lives when they are beginning to form their own identity and
> social groups. But, she says, parents should not worry. Studies
> have shown that parents are more influential in their teens'
> lives than the teens' peers and that parents have more con-
> trol over their teenagers than they think they do. The key for
> parents, de Guzman says, is to communicate with their teens
> and work through conflicts. Peer friendships are often posi-
> tive experiences and help young people develop healthy friend-
> ships and learn about social norms.

A dolescence is a time when peers play an increasingly important role in the lives of youth. Teens begin to develop
friendships that are more intimate, exclusive, and more con-
stant than in earlier years. In many ways, these friendships are
an essential component of development. They provide safe venues

Maria R.T. de Guzman, "Friendships, Peer Influence, and Peer Pressure During the Teen Years," *NebGuide*, August 2007. Reproduced by permission of University of Nebraska–Lincoln Extension, Institute of Agriculture and Natural Resources.

Types of Peer Pressure

Peer pressure can take many forms. For example:

- Pressure to dress the same way
- Pressure to dye hair
- Pressure to have ears pierced
- Pressure to listen to the same music
- Pressure to change clothing styles
- Pressure to hang out later
- Pressure to change your look
- Pressure to cut your hair

Taken from: Growing Kids, www.growingkids.co.uk/DealingWithPeerPressure.html.

where youth can explore their identities, where they can feel accepted and where they can develop a sense of belongingness. Friendships also allow youth to practice and foster social skills necessary for future success.

Nonetheless, parents and other adults can become concerned when they see their teens becoming preoccupied with their friends. Many parents worry that their teens might fall under negative peer influence or reject their families' values and beliefs, as well as be pressured to engage in high-risk and other negative behaviors.

In actuality, peer influence is more complex than our stereotype of the negative influences from friends. First, peer influence can be both positive and negative. While we tend to think that peer influence leads teens to engage in unhealthy and unsafe behaviors, it can actually motivate youth to study harder in school, volunteer for community and social services, and participate in sports and other productive endeavors. In fact, most teens report that their peers pressure them not to engage in drug use and sexual activity.

Second, peer influence is not a simple process where youth are passive recipients of influence from others. In fact, peers who become friends tend to already have a lot of things in common. Peers with similar interests [and] similar academic standing [who] enjoy doing the same things tend to gravitate towards each other. So while it seems that teens and their friends become very similar to each other through peer influence, much of that similarity was present to begin with.

Facts About Friendships, Peers, and Adolescence

Friendships that emerge during adolescence tend to be more complex, more exclusive, and more consistent than during earlier childhood. New types (e.g., opposite sex, romantic ties) and levels (e.g., best friends, cliques, and "crowds") of relationships emerge, and teens begin to develop the capacity for very close, intimate, and deep friendships.

The adult perception of peers as having one culture or a unified front of dangerous influence is inaccurate. More often than not, peers reinforce family values, but they have the potential to encourage problem behaviors as well. Although the negative peer influence is overemphasized, more can be done to help teenagers experience the family and the peer group as mutually constructive environments.

Facts About the Teen-Parent Relationship

- **Parent relationships are not necessarily undermined by peer relationships.** During adolescence, relationships between parents and teens are more often re-negotiated rather than rejected. During adolescence, teens become increasingly autonomous and take on more adult roles. They also develop their own ideas and start mapping their own lives. They begin to spend more time with and value their friends more than they used to. Thus, it might seem as if they are starting to cut ties with parents and reject their ideals. In fact, rather than cutting off ties, teens are just renegotiating the parent-child relationship.

What this means is that they are beginning to shift the relationship to incorporate their increasing independence and maturity. As teens become more mature, the type of relationship they have with their parents naturally begins to shift as the teen begins to mature.

- **While it seems that teens are influenced by their peers, parents continue to be the most influential factor in their lives.** Despite fears parents have about their teens rejecting their values and beliefs, parents continue to be of significant influence. Teens report having political, religious, and general beliefs similar to their parents' and consider their parents as being highly significant and influential in their lives. Positive relationships between parents and teens also equip youth to have healthy relationships with friends. Teens who have high quality relationships with parents also report having a positive relationship with their peers.

- **Parent-adolescent conflict increases between childhood and early adolescence; although in most families, its frequency and intensity remain low.** Typically, conflicts are the result of relationship negotiation and continuing attempts by parents to socialize their adolescents, and do not signal the breakdown of parent-adolescent relations. Parents need to include adolescents in decision-making and rule-setting that affects their lives.

- **Parents who continue to communicate with their teens, even when there are conflicts, actually maintain closer relationships.** While it might seem futile to talk to teens when it leads to conflicts and disagreements, most teens continue to report having a close relationship with their parents, and as mentioned earlier, they still report parents as being a significant influence on their lives. So parents

Studies have shown that parents who continue to communicate with their teens maintain closer relationships even when conflict within the family occurs.

need to continue talking to their teens and maintaining an open line of communication, rather than simply trying to avoid disagreements.

Facts About Peer Friendships

- **Teens often have multiple layers and groups of friendships.** Unlike in childhood, when friendships usually meant two or more close friends, teens often have multiple friends and belong to multiple groups. They might have intimate and close relationships with one or a handful of individuals, and might also belong to one or more "cliques" or groups of friends that have similar demographics (sex, race, socioeconomic status), orientation towards school, and other interests.
- **Peer friendships are dynamic.** This simply means that peer friendships may change. For instance, while teens can have friendships that are long term, they often move from one clique to another, and they might develop new friendships and lose others.
- **Peers tend to choose those who are similar to themselves.** Whether it is gender, age, socioeconomic status, ethnicity, or interests, teens tend to gravitate towards those who are more similar to them.
- **Peer friendships can be a healthy venue for positive youth development.** Peer friendships can be a safe place for youth to explore their identity, learn about social norms, and practice their autonomy. Healthy friendships provide youth with social support for dealing with some of the challenges of adolescence, and can also provide youth with some of the most positive experiences during those years. Many teens report having some of the happiest and most fun moments with their peers, likely due to shared interests as well as close relationships.

Effective Strategies for Coping with Peer Pressure

While the point has been made here that peer influence and peer pressure do not necessarily have to be negative, peer pressure can lead youth towards unhealthy and unsafe behaviors. To minimize the negative effects of peer pressure, youth, parents, school and community leaders must come together to establish workable and effective strategies to guide teen behavior and to support their transition from children to mature, responsible adults. Here are several strategies to consider:

1. **Nurture teens' abilities and self-esteem so that they are equipped to foster positive peer relationships and deflect negative pressures.** Adolescents with positive self-concept and self-worth will be less likely to be easily swayed to follow others' negative influences. It is essential that these aspects of positive development should be encouraged in youth.

2. **Encourage positive relationships between significant adults and teens.** Parents, teachers, school counselors, other relatives and professionals should try to have constructive and positive relationships with teens. These can serve as good models for healthy relationships, and can be a venue through which the teens can feel valued and where they can develop positive views about themselves. Youth should know that they can go to these caring adults for help or advice about their peer relationships.

3. **Encourage diverse relationships.** Parents, teachers, community leaders, and clergy can model appreciation for ethnic, gender, socioeconomic status, religious, and other differences and support cross-group friendships. Schools and youth organizations can assist by encouraging youth from diverse backgrounds to work and play together.

4. **Support parent education programs for families with teenagers.** Parents need to be better informed about the dynamics of adolescent peer groups and the demands and expectations teenagers face in peer relationships. Information is available through various sources including books, some parenting magazines, and other publications such as this one. Keep your eye out for programs particularly targeted towards families and teen issues that might be available. Seeking information is not a sign of weakness, and

showing interest in these issues might actually show your teens that you are concerned about them.

5. **Equip youth with the skills necessary to resist negative behaviors, as well as to make good decisions.** Teens will inevitably be confronted with situations where they will have to make a decision whether or not to engage in certain behaviors, whether to give in to peer pressure, and also to make other difficult decisions. It is essential that youth are given the necessary skills to analyze the situation and make the appropriate decision. This includes helping youth develop the skills for "costs vs. benefits" analysis—teaching them to look at both the negative and positive sides to making a decision. For instance, if being pressured to smoke, the teen should be able to think about what the possible desired outcomes are (e.g., peer acceptance, looking "cool," feeling excitement about trying something new) with the possible undesirable outcomes (e.g., becoming hooked, the health issues, smelling bad, the financial costs).

6. **Teaching youth exit strategies or ways to say "no" to negative pressures.** It is best to try to deal with peer pressure before it even happens. Talk to youth about potential scenarios, and think through strategies together on how to deal with those scenarios if they arise. This could be done by discussing hypothetical scenarios or even role-playing. It is helpful to think about these things ahead of time rather than dealing with situations as they occur or trying to recover after they happen.

Deflect Negative Peer Pressure

During adolescence, peers play a large part in a young person's life even while the family continues to be significant. In general, peer friendships offer youth many positive opportunities despite the negative connotations that peer relationships have to many of us. Peer relationships are actually important for healthy development and essential for youth to develop into healthy adults.

Nonetheless, peer relationships also have the potential to encourage problem behaviors. Although the negative influence of peers is often over-emphasized, more can be done to help teenagers experience the family and the peer group as mutually constructive environments. To accomplish this, families, communities, churches, schools, 4-H and other youth groups can all contribute to helping youth develop positive peer relationships, and deflect negative peer pressures and influences.

TWO

Risky Teen Behavior May Be Linked to Brain Development

Sharon Jayson

> Sharon Jayson is a reporter and journalist for radio, television, and print. In the following viewpoint she reports that brain researchers have found that the brains of adolescents are not yet fully developed and that teens do not have the capacity to avoid risky behavior. The portion of the brain that regulates impulse, logic, reasoning, and emotion is not fully developed until after the age of eighteen. According to Jayson, researchers say that education programs and intervention strategies aimed at persuading teens against risky behaviors are wasted because adolescents are not entirely able to control their actions, especially when they are in the company of peers. Rather, Jayson reports, more effort and money should be put into raising the driving age to eighteen, increasing the price of cigarettes, and enforcing underage drinking laws.

A new review of adolescent brain research suggests that society is wasting billions of dollars on education and intervention programs to dissuade teens from dangerous activities, because their immature brains are not yet capable of avoiding risky behaviors.

The analysis, by Temple University psychologist Laurence Steinberg, says stricter laws and policies limiting their behaviors would be more effective than education programs.

"We need to rethink our whole approach to preventing teen risk," says Steinberg, whose review of a decade of research is in the April [2007] issue of *Current Directions in Psychological Science*. It's published by the Association for Psychological Science.

"Adolescents are at an age where they do not have full capacity to control themselves," he says. "As adults, we need to do some of the controlling."

Peer Pressure Rules

Neurological researchers around the country, spearheaded by Jay Giedd of the National Institute of Mental Health, have in recent years found that the brain is not fully developed until after 18.

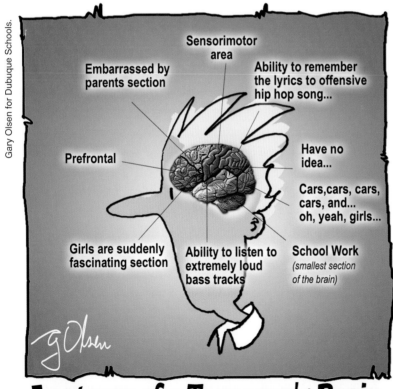

Gary Olsen for Dubuque Schools.

Sensorimotor area

Embarrassed by parents section

Ability to remember the lyrics to offensive hip hop song...

Prefrontal

Have no idea...

Cars, cars, cars, cars, and... oh, yeah, girls...

Girls are suddenly fascinating section

Ability to listen to extremely loud bass tracks

School Work (smallest section of the brain)

Anatomy of a Teenager's Brain

The brain system that regulates logic and reasoning develops before the area that regulates impulse and emotions, the researchers say.

Studies by Steinberg and others have found that the mere physical presence of peers increased the likelihood of teens taking risks.

Now he's using brain imaging to better understand why teens are so susceptible to peer pressure. He has just begun pilot projects to study brain activity in teens when doing various tasks with their peers, compared with adults under similar circumstances.

Steinberg believes raising the driving age, increasing the price of cigarettes and more strongly enforcing underage drinking laws are among ways to really curb risky behavior.

"I don't believe the problem behind teen risky behavior is a lack of knowledge. The programs do a good job in teaching kids the facts," he says. "Education alone doesn't work. It doesn't seem to affect their behavior."

Michael Bradley, a Philadelphia-area psychologist and author specializing in teenagers, says U.S. culture tends to view teens as small adults when, neurologically, they are large children.

"Kids will sign drug pledges. They really mean that, but when they get in a park on a Friday night with their friends, that pledge is nowhere to be found in their brain structure. They're missing the neurologic brakes that adults have."

Bradley also is worried about the future now that risky behaviors have trickled to the preteen set.

"People look at risk statistics, and they're more or less steady. It looks like things aren't getting that bad. But risk behaviors have been ratcheted down to younger and younger ages," he says. "What the parents may have dealt with at ages 16 and 17, the kids are dealing with at 11, 12 and 13—at the time when their brains are least able to handle complex decisions about risk behaviors."

Raise the Driving Age

Such policy talk—even from psychologists—sparks a useful conversation, says Isabel Sawhill, co-director of the Center on Children and Families at the Washington-based Brookings Institution.

Because studies have shown that the brain is not fully developed until adulthood, some experts contend that the driving age for teens should be raised.

"It is good research for policymakers to consider, but we shouldn't infer from this research that all our past efforts have been ineffective," she says. "I'm not in favor of just doing education, but I'm also not in favor of *not* doing it, either. We need to do some of both."

Experts such as Sawhill and Caterina Roman, a senior research associate at the Washington-based Urban Institute, say some educational programs do work. But the widely popular Drug Abuse Resistance Education program known as DARE, launched in the 1980s, was determined to be ineffective.

Roman believes that recent findings that the teen brain is not yet fully developed will spawn some of the restrictions Steinberg recommends.

"Ten years from now, the driving age will be higher than it is now. The price of cigarettes will increase," she predicts.

Steinberg says he's not advocating a police state. But he says parents must help their children make wise decisions.

"We've given them too much freedom," he says. "We don't monitor and supervise them carefully enough."

THREE

Sturdier Brain Networks May Help Children Resist Peer Pressure

Tom Valeo

Tom Valeo writes about medical issues for the Dana Foundation's *BrainWork*, *The Boston Globe*, *Scientific American*, and *Chicago* magazine. He also writes a column on aging for *The St. Petersburg Times*. In the following viewpoint Valeo reports on startling new research into brain development. Researchers at the University of Nottingham in England have found that during adolescence, the frontal lobes of the brain develop and grow rapidly and communicate with other regions of the brain, such as those that control higher-level decision making, impulse control, and judgment. The networks that govern goal-oriented activity are separated in adults, whereas they are merged in children, separating over time during the adolescent years. In a test to determine resistance to peer pressure, children who responded strongly to angry facial expressions displayed less self-monitoring and impulse control. Children who have trouble controlling their impulses are more likely to respond inappropriately to peer pressure.

Children who have a greater ability to resist peer pressure also have stronger connections among regions in their frontal

Tom Valeo, "Sturdier Brain Networks May Help Children Resist Peer Pressure," The Dana Foundation, September 19, 2007. Reproduced by permission.

lobes and other brain areas, according to a study conducted by Tomáš Paus at the University of Nottingham in England.

Bradley L. Schlaggar, who has done his own research on brain development, called the study "interesting, novel and provocative."

"I don't think there was any anticipation that such an investigation would yield such clear results," said Schlaggar, assistant professor of pediatrics, radiology, neurology, and neurobiology and anatomy at Washington University School of Medicine in St. Louis.

During adolescence, the frontal lobes of the brain undergo rapid development, with the axons in that region gaining a coat of fatty myelin, which insulates them, facilitating the transmission of signals. This enables the frontal lobes to communicate more effectively with other brain regions and incorporate those signals into higher-level decision making. This type of "executive control" over impulses and perceptions originating in other parts of the brain gradually produces the judgment, self-control and analytical ability characteristic of adults—and important for resisting peer influence.

This computer graphic of the human brain shows the frontal lobes in yellow and green. Children with stronger connections among the regions of the brain have a better ability to resist peer pressure.

Tests for Lower Impulse Control

To determine who was better able to resist peer influence, Paus presented 46 10-year-olds a series of questions and statements such as, "I worry what others think of me," along with giving them behavioral tests and an intelligence test. Then 35 of the children took turns lying in a functional magnetic resonance imaging (fMRI) scanner, watching video images of hands manipulating a phone, pencil and other objects in either a neutral way or an angry way as the scanner took images of their brain activity. While in the scanner, they also watched videos of facial expressions that changed from neutral to angry.

Children who recorded a stronger reaction to angry movements and facial expressions while in the machine scored lower on those interview statements and questions that measured their resistance to peer influence. They also displayed less self-monitoring while taking other tests and scored lower on tests of impulse control.

These findings, reported in the *Journal of Neuroscience* in July [2007], are important "if we are to understand how the adolescent brain attains the right balance between acknowledging the influences of others and maintaining one's independence," Paus said in a statement about the work.

He plans to do follow-up studies with these children to determine if these differences in brain connectivity predict which children later will display greater resistance to real-life peer influence.

Impaired Impulse Control and Peer Pressure

Schlaggar co-authored a study published in June [2007] that revealed how coordinated networks of brain activity in adults govern most goal-oriented activity, including reading, listening to music or searching for a pattern. However, these networks appear to be merged in children and to separate only gradually during adolescence. Understanding this change may lead to a better understanding of conditions of impaired impulse control, such as Tourette's syndrome and attention-deficit disorder, Schlaggar said.

The Paus study points to the importance of self-regulation, Schlaggar said. "Your sense of yourself and how you relate to others is

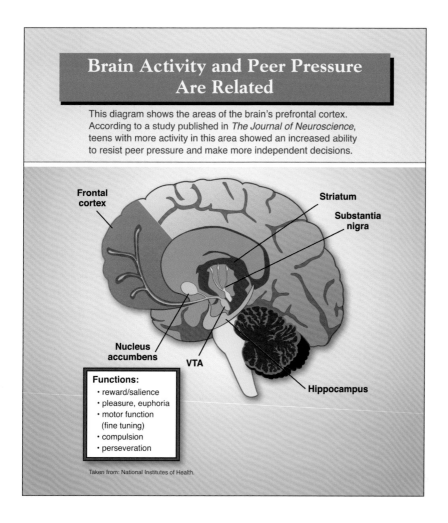

Brain Activity and Peer Pressure Are Related

This diagram shows the areas of the brain's prefrontal cortex. According to a study published in *The Journal of Neuroscience*, teens with more activity in this area showed an increased ability to resist peer pressure and make more independent decisions.

Frontal cortex

Striatum

Substantia nigra

Nucleus accumbens

VTA

Hippocampus

Functions:
- reward/salience
- pleasure, euphoria
- motor function (fine tuning)
- compulsion
- perseveration

Taken from: National Institutes of Health.

going to fall under the category of executive control or impulse control," he said. "Individuals who have trouble controlling their impulses will be most likely to respond inappropriately to peer influence."

In Schlaggar's opinion, studies such as this that use fMRI and other imaging techniques to link brain functions to real-world behavior will help shed light on the brain's role in everyday problems—such as the potential negative effect of peer influence.

"The development of temperament, emotional regulation and social interaction in adolescents is a field that needs a lot of attention," he said. "This kind of approach will help bring disciplines together to help understand the basic mechanisms of emotional and cognitive development."

FOUR

Peer Pressure Can Impact Eating and Exercise Habits

Sally Squires

Sally Squires is the health and nutrition columnist for *The Washington Post*. In the following viewpoint she reports on studies that show peer pressure can affect body image, weight, bingeing, and the development of eating disorders. Researchers at the University of Miami studied various self-titled groups of teens, such as the popular kids, jocks, brains, burnouts, and alternatives. Results, published in the *Journal of Youth and Adolescence*, found that girls in the burnout and alternative peer groups were more likely to have low body image, be more weight conscious, and take steps to control their weight. On the bright side, studies show that teens who have regular meals at home with their family are less likely to develop eating disorders.

Television, movies, magazines and other popular media often get blamed for pressuring teen girls to be as thin as models. But a new study finds that peer pressure also plays a strong role in how some adolescent girls control their figures.

This isn't the first time that peer pressure has been fingered as a factor in risky teen behavior. Other studies have found that the cliques with which many teens identify can affect whether they smoke, drink or take drugs. It now appears that similar identification carries weight when it comes to body image, food and physical activity.

"Teen girls' concerns about their own weight, about how they appear to others and their perceptions that their peers want them to be thin are significantly related to weight-control behavior," says psychologist Eleanor Mackey, a postdoctoral fellow at Children's National Medical Center and lead author of the study. "Those are really important."

Estimates are that about 5 percent of teens suffer from eating disorders, including anorexia nervosa, a condition characterized by not eating, and bulimia, eating and then purging. A study published

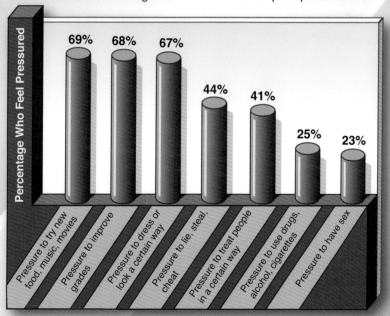

Peer Pressure Is Real

Teenagers who visited the SmartGirl Web site participated in an online survey concerning peer pressure. The results showed that a large number of teens felt peer pressure.

Percentage Who Feel Pressured

- Pressure to try new food, music, movies — 69%
- Pressure to improve grades — 68%
- Pressure to dress or look a certain way — 67%
- Pressure to lie, steal, cheat — 44%
- Pressure to treat people in a certain way — 41%
- Pressure to use drugs, alcohol, cigarettes — 25%
- Pressure to have sex — 23%

Taken from: "Report on Peer Pressure," SmartGirl, www.smartgirl.org/reports/1866433.html.

[in June 2008] in the *Archives of Pediatric and Adolescent Medicine* found that 10 percent of teen girls and about 3 percent of teen boys binge-eat at least once a week.

At the same time, about a third of adolescents are overweight, while about 16 percent are obese, according to the federal Centers for Disease Control and Prevention. Those added pounds place them at increased risk for a host of health problems, including Type 2 diabetes, high blood pressure and heart disease.

Study Measures Peer Influence and Body Image

To measure the role of peer pressure on eating and exercise habits, Mackey and co-author Annette M. La Greca of the University of Miami studied 236 teen girls from public high schools in southeast Florida. About a third were white; about a third were Hispanic or Latino, and roughly 20 percent were African American. The remainder were of mixed ethnicity.

All completed questionnaires probing their identification with informal but well-documented teen groupings labeled "populars" (those who are outgoing and social), "brains" (teens who enjoy school and do well academically), "burnouts" (adolescents who often get into trouble), "jocks" (those who engage in sports) and "alternatives" (teens who rebel against mainstream culture in their appearance and attitudes).

Participants answered questions about body image and weight control as well as how others appraised their appearance.

The study, which appears in [the July 2008] *Journal of Youth and Adolescence*, found that:

- Girls who identified with the alternative and burnout peer groups were the most worried about their weight and reported taking more steps than other groups to control it, sometimes in potentially unhealthy ways.
- Participants with a higher body mass index perceived their peers to be more concerned with weight than their thinner counterparts. They also reported engaging in more dieting and other steps to control their weight than their more svelte peers.

Teen girls' perceptions about their own weight and how others see them are significantly related to weight-control behavior.

- African American girls were less concerned about their weight than were others.

A 2007 study by the same researchers found that teens most likely to identify with the burnout group had the worst eating, exercise and weight-control behavior of all the groups. So-called brains had the best eating and workout regimens, though they also reported more dieting than other teens. Jocks and populars didn't always eat healthfully but were the most likely to get plenty of exercise and to engage in sports.

Identify Peer Groups to Help Girls at Risk

The findings offer guidance in targeting girls who might be most vulnerable to weight issues. "Health-care providers and school personnel might ask adolescent girls about their peer crowd affiliations in order to help identify adolescents with the highest levels of risky behaviors," the authors conclude.

What also seems to help build healthy eating habits in teens is encouraging family meals, according to Project Eating Among Teens [Project EAT], a long-term study of nearly 5,000 adolescents and their families conducted at the University of Minnesota.

The research finds that family meals are linked to better diets, including more fruit and vegetables, less soda and less dietary fat, according to Dianne Neumark-Sztainer, a professor of epidemiology at the University of Minnesota School of Public Health and a lead investigator of Project EAT.

Children from families that regularly break bread together also seem to have a lower risk of developing eating disorders such as anorexia and bulimia. They're less likely to be overweight. They perform better in school and are less apt to engage in risky behavior such as taking drugs, drinking, smoking and engaging in sex.

FIVE

Popular Teens Are Susceptible to Peer Pressure

Charlotte Crystal

> Charlotte Crystal writes for *Inside University of Virginia*. In the following viewpoint Crystal reports on a study that reveals that popular students are uniquely susceptible to peer pressure and engage in risky behavior, such as smoking or shoplifting, because they want to follow the crowd. Despite this, popular kids also showed strong family attachments and a sense of personal identity. However, teens who succumb to peer pressure or minor deviant behavior are not destined for a life of crime in their adult lives. Teens eventually move away from delinquent behavior as they get older and are able to think on their own.

Being a popular teenager can be a risky business. On one hand, they have a lot of friends. On the other hand, they're particularly vulnerable to these friends leading them astray.

That was one of several conclusions drawn by a team of researchers led by psychology professor Joseph P. Allen. The research results of "The Two Faces of Adolescents' Success with Peers: Adolescent Popularity, Social Adaptation, and Deviant Behavior," was published in the May/June 2005 issue of *Child Development* released on May 17.

Teens study together, an example of the positive aspects of peer pressure that support maintaining good relationships with peers.

The good news is that the popular teens in the study showed strong family attachments and a healthy sense of personal identity. The bad news is that their ability to get along well with others makes them particularly susceptible to following friends into such risky activities as shoplifting or smoking marijuana.

"Our study looked at popularity among teenagers both as a measure of good social skills and as a risk factor for doing things their parents wouldn't like, things that could get the kids into trouble," Allen said.

The study also found some positive effects of peer socialization, in terms of pressure to get along well with others.

Adolescents Maintain Positive Relationships with Peers

"While early adolescent norms may support challenging adult rules and norms, these norms also tend to support behaviors that maintain positive relationships with peers," the researchers found. "Behaviors such as hostile aggression toward peers, which meet with broad disapproval within adolescent peer groups and which decrease in frequency over time in adolescence, might be expected to be socialized out of popular adolescents' behavioral repertoires."

Researchers worked with 185 seventh- and eighth-graders in Charlottesville, Va. Of the pupils interviewed, 87 were male and 98 were female. The pupils who chose to participate, with parental

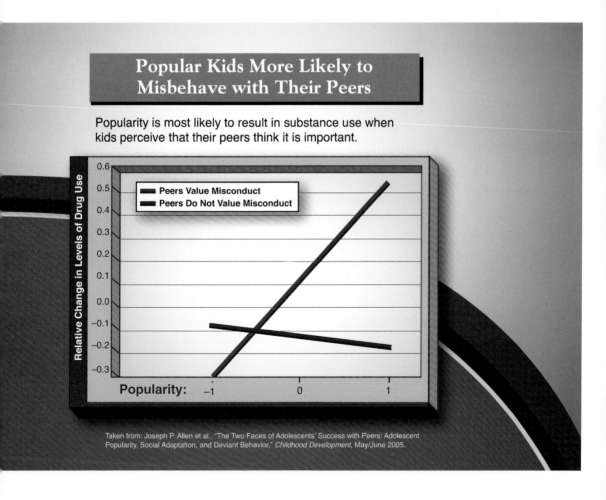

Popular Kids More Likely to Misbehave with Their Peers

Popularity is most likely to result in substance use when kids perceive that their peers think it is important.

Taken from: Joseph P. Allen et al., "The Two Faces of Adolescents' Success with Peers: Adolescent Popularity, Social Adaptation, and Deviant Behavior," *Childhood Development*, May/June 2005.

permission, were interviewed along with their mothers and close friends about whom they would most like to spend time with on a Saturday night. The sample was racially and socio-economically diverse: 58 percent Caucasian, 29 percent African American, and 13 percent who identified themselves as "other" or of mixed racial or ethnic parentage. The median income of the sample families was $40,000–$59,999, with 18 percent reporting family incomes of less than $20,000 and 33 percent reporting incomes of more than $60,000. Data was gathered in two waves, in 1998 and 2000.

Along with Allen, the researchers included Maryfrances R. Porter and F. Christy McFarland, U.Va [University of Virginia] doctoral candidates in clinical psychology; Penny Marsh, a doctoral student in psychology at the University of Washington; and Kathleen Boykin McElhaney, adjunct assistant professor of psychology at Davidson College.

The study is funded by the National Institute of Mental Health. An original grant of $1.5 million in 1998 was followed by a subsequent five-year grant of $3 million, which ends in 2008. The original participants in this longitudinal study will be 23 when the current funding ends, though Allen hopes to secure additional funding to follow them further.

Deviant Behavior Not Likely to Last a Lifetime

The silver lining is that "minor deviant behavior" by popular teens is not likely to lead them to "serious levels of deviant behavior," i.e., to commit serious crimes, or even to sustain minor levels of deviance over long periods of time, the researchers found. They suggested more study to learn whether popular teens move away from delinquent behavior as the prevailing norms in their peer groups change, or whether, as they grow older and more able to think on their own, they are less easily influenced by their peer groups.

Among the heartening conclusions: Peers matter, but so do parents. The same traits that lead kids to be popular with their peers, lead them to ask for guidance from their parents.

"Parents need to keep talking with their teens," Allen said.

SIX

Organized Activities Can Deter Negative Peer Behavior

Thorolfur Thorlindsson and Jon Gunnar Bernburg

Thorolfur Thorlindsson and Jon Gunnar Bernburg are members of the Faculty of Social Science at the University of Iceland, Reykjavik. Thorlindsson was also a visiting professor at the Department of Sociology and Anthropology at North Carolina State University. In the following viewpoint Thorlindsson and Bernburg discuss their study on how organized activities such as sports and social groups can keep teens from engaging in risky behaviors. Findings also showed that even if youths have drug-using peers, they are less likely to engage in substance use the more they themselves are involved with sports.

The peer group is the center of the adolescent life-world. Adolescents spend more time with their peers than they do with their parents or alone. . . . The development of a global youth culture has at the same time provided new opportunities to promote the use of alcohol and drugs among adolescents.

Peers can enforce or challenge the norms and authority of adult society. On the one hand, research indicates that having deviant friends is a major source of risk-taking and delinquent behavior. Thus criminologists argue that association with deviant

Thorolfur Thorlindsson and Jon Gunnar Bernburg, "Peer Groups and Substance Use: Examining the Direct and Interactive Effect of Leisure Activity," *Adolescence*, vol. 41, Summer 2006, pp. 321–39. Copyright © 2006 Libra Publishers, Inc. Reproduced by permission.

peers leads to deviance through mechanisms of social learning, peer pressure, and transference of deviant attitudes and values. On the other hand, youth researchers have paid attention to the positive aspects of youth culture, pointing out that participation in youth leisure activities often provides adolescents with valuable experience.

Youth Leisure Activity

Participating in adolescent activities can expand horizons, offer opportunities to develop skills, and foster a sense of acceptance and belonging. Research suggests that youth activities can provide a context in which adolescents are emotionally and cognitively engaged in exploring identities, enhancing social skills and personal development. There is also a body of research which suggests that participation in extracurricular activities is positively related to academic performance, psychological well-being, and self-esteem, but negatively related to substance use. . . .

Consequently, this article blends ideas and concepts from criminology and youth leisure research to examine the association between youth peer cultures and substance use. We assume that having fun, seeking excitement, and challenging adult society, are essential characteristics of peer group activities. . . . Adolescents from all walks of life are members of a leisure class characterized by weakened social control, especially on the part of parents and the school. At the same time, adolescents are free from the demands of self-support and the integrative bonds of work and marriage, giving them the freedom to seek leisure without the adult responsibilities. . . .

In line with the youth research literature, we emphasize the diversity of peer culture and peer lifestyle and the importance of the peer group in promoting various kinds of behavior. But we argue that some forms of leisure activity may help integrate adolescents into society and enable them to reach shared societal goals, whereas other activities may foster subcultures that challenge the normative consensus of conventional adult society. Classifying and comparing youth leisure activities across domains with reference to specific outcomes may help us gain a better understanding of peer group influence.

Three Popular Peer Activities

We identify three types of highly popular peer activities that offer alternative ways of forming and organizing peer subcultures, having fun, and seeking excitement. The first leisure pattern involves sport participation. In recent years, an expanding group of social scientists have generated a considerable body of knowledge about sport subcultures. Building on this research, we argue that participation in sport can provide a social context that is characterized by distinguishing patterns of values, norms and rituals, and practices that shape the behavior of its participants. . . . The second leisure pattern involves activities that consist mainly of hanging

Youth participation in sports can provide a social context for patterns of values and norms that shape a teen's behavior.

out and going to parties. . . . The "party subculture" is intertwined with contemporary popular culture. It is central in the lives of adolescents and is characterized by the subterranean values that pervade the contemporary popular culture. The third leisure pattern is characterized by participation in adult supervised and/or organized leisure, promoted by social youth clubs. Youth clubs offer the opportunity to have fun with peers, socialize, dance and listen to music in an adult-guided environment. . . .

Social Bonding Weakens Deviant Peer Behavior

We expect involvement in sport and youth clubs to be negatively associated with substance use while involvement in the party subculture should be positively associated with substance use. Aside from the direct effects of leisure pattern involvement, we argue that differential leisure pattern involvement may condition the well-documented relationship between adolescent deviance and associating with deviant peers. Deviance and crime researchers have shown that social bonding to conventional institutions, such as the family, the school, and religion, weaken the effect of deviant peer association on adolescent deviance. We expect involvement in sports and youth clubs to have similar protective effects. Thus, we hypothesize that the statistical influence of substance-using peers on substance use should decrease with a higher level of involvement in sports and youth clubs. Conversely, we expect that the statistical influence of having substance-using friends should increase with a higher level of involvement in the party subculture. . . .

Involvement in Sports Deters Alcohol and Drug Use

Our findings highlight the fact that peer groups formed on the basis of leisure activity can function as agents that deter alcohol and drug use even if the individual has close contact with drug-using peers. The findings reveal that adolescents who engage in leisure activities such as sports and organized club activity are less likely to use alcohol and drugs. More importantly, the findings indicate that the influence of associating with alcohol- and drug-using peers on substance use becomes significantly weaker with greater involvement in sports and clubs. These findings hold when other important factors related to family and school are controlled for.

These findings underline the importance of leisure activity for adolescents in terms of prevention in contemporary society. Both our findings and the wider social context strongly suggest that promoting youth sport and organized leisure as alternatives to association with alcohol- and drug-using peer groups should help reduce

Peer Pressure to Use Drugs Declines as Teens Age

Children in Glasgow, Scotland, who participated in a study gave reasons for their use of drugs. Results show that peer pressure to use drugs is higher for younger children (ages 10–12) than for children ages 11–14. As teens age, they more often cite reasons such as boredom and personal choice for using drugs.

Reason for Using Drugs	Children Ages 10–12	Children Ages 11–14
Curiosity	65 percent	82 percent
Peer pressure	26 percent	5 percent
Encouragement/reassurance	22 percent	14 percent
Desire to conform	16 percent	9 percent
Boredom	16 percent	18 percent

Taken from: J. McIntosh, F. MacDonald, and N. McKeganey, "Why Do Children Experiment with Illegal Drugs? The Declining Role of Peer Pressure with Increasing Age," *Addiction Research and Theory*, June 2006.

alcohol and drug use among adolescents. Sport provides a particularly interesting avenue for preventive work. A majority of adolescents at one time or another participate in organized sport. It is highly structured and is practiced in an institutionalized context in clubs or in relation to school. The existing sport networks among youth are quite large and could be activated for prevention purposes. Given the importance of sport in the life of young people, it is somewhat surprising how little attention it has received in the effort to reduce adolescents' alcohol and substance use. Alcohol producers have certainly recognized the opportunities for influencing adolescents through sport. They have targeted sport events, promoting the sport and advertising beer and liquor at the same time.

The Entertainment Industry Promotes a Culture of Fun

As the adolescent society becomes more independent from the adult society of parents and school, it becomes easier for market forces to influence adolescents directly. They can create a youth culture that promotes fun and consumption in one form or another. The entertainment industry is not very likely to promote parental or educational goals unless it benefits them directly. They are, in fact, more likely to encourage the emergence of subterranean values among adolescents. A more salient international and commercially driven youth culture that is becoming more independent of the local adult society, combined with the fact that adolescents already spend more time with their peers than they do with parents, is a trend that preventive work needs to take seriously.

On a more general level these findings strongly indicate the importance for anyone interested in the welfare of young people to pay close attention to adolescent peer culture and lifestyle. If the present trend continues, adolescent leisure activities and peer culture will probably be even more important in the near future. The weakening of social control leaves today's youth more free to seek excitement and fun, form subcultures, and develop lifestyles which are in contrast to the dominating adult culture. The emergence of international, commercially driven popular youth cultures makes the peer group particularly salient in the life of young people. Social changes that have occurred in the last fifty years have shifted the balance of power from traditional institutions such as the family, church, and school to the market. The entertainment industry, heavily geared toward peers, offers adolescents more freedom to choose lifestyles, values, and norms outside the direct guidance and control of family and school, strengthening the peer group's position at the center of the adolescent life-world. It provides global markets that have been heavily targeted by the entertainment and fashion industry that promotes the culture of fun and excitement and fosters unrealistic expectations.

As peers become more autonomous and influential, parents and educators become more concerned about the power of the peer group in promoting deviant and risk-taking behaviors. At the same time, attention should be turned toward the diversity that exists in peer groups. It seems inadequate to deal with the wide range of leisure activities within this age group as if it represented homogeneous peer cultures and lifestyles.

SEVEN

Parents Can Help Teens Resist Peer Pressure

Elizabeth Hartley-Brewer

> Elizabeth Hartley-Brewer is an adviser on children's learning and development and the author of *Talking to Tweens* and *Raising Happy Kids*. In the following viewpoint she explains that around age eight children gravitate away from parents and teachers and toward their friends. They follow their friends' lead, wanting the same clothes and music. Parents need to stand firmly when setting rules of conduct and refuse to buy the hottest new electronics or clothes. Tweens, Hartley-Brewer contends, will actually see parental rules as a form of love, that parents are taking an interest in their lives. Parents should not be afraid to say no, must be firm but show compassion and understanding, and must show that they are in charge but also be flexible and allow children to grow and learn.

My two children nearly badgered me to death in their pre-teen years. They were desperate to fit in and were furious when I refused them what they wanted. Being a middle-school teacher made it a little easier to say no. I had learned that at about age 8, students stop soaking up their teacher's every word and follow their friends instead. I had also seen how quickly tweens get over (and forget) things that only a short time before had been among life's greatest disappointments or injustices. But still, I admit to feeling pleased when my daughter later declared, "It was good you wouldn't let me have a GameBoy. My friends waste so much time on them." And I'm probably not the only mother whose teenage son thanked her for not allowing him to get an earring when he was 10, because it wasn't "like, cool, now."

What to Expect

For many parents, the scariest part of the tween years is that it's the beginning of the end of your total control. When your child is younger, you're the ultimate "decider." At about age 8, however, the power starts to shift as your child spends more time with his peers, experiments, and becomes his own person. Most significantly

Many parents find their child's tween years difficult because they begin to lose power over their child's decisions.

during the tween years, your child will want to prove that he's capable of being different from you (which, of course, he is), and as a result, he will become more likely to assert himself, even if it causes conflict.

You'll probably find that your 8-, 9-, or 10-year-old daughter will want to dress in the sexy teen fashions that are now marketed to younger children. Your 10- or 11-year-old son will play music that offends your ears and your taste. And older tweens will beg you to let them pierce their ears or belly buttons or buy them the latest cell phone, MP3 player, TV, or computer, despite the fact that the one they already have works just fine. Any tween is likely to want to watch movies or play video games that are rated above his chronological age because "everyone" else is doing so.

Even more difficult than being pestered by your child to buy a particular item because it's the current fad is having your values challenged. As the mom of one 10-year-old put it, "My daughter is now aware that there's another world out there. She sees that other families do things differently, and she prefers their way because she thinks there's more in it for her. It can be hard to stick to your principles in the face of the pressure." But it's important to do so as best you can. Although you understandably want to please your child, giving in is not helpful to her in the long- or short-term.

How You Can Help

The inevitable battles you have with your tween can actually boost his sense of being loved and cared for, if handled sensitively. However angry your child may be at the time of your refusal, deep down he will prefer having a parent who has his best interests at heart and who has clear and consistent principles. A parent who frequently bends and then gives in to a child's demands is less able to provide him with that beneficial sense of security and clarity.

Don't be afraid to say no. Experiencing disappointment and learning that one can survive happily without a "must-have" item or activity is a necessary part of growing up. While such experiences may be painful to your child in the moment, they will ultimately help strengthen his self-esteem. Conversely, always giving your child what he wants may seem like the way to ensure his happiness, but it often ends up feeding his anxiety, and encourages him to define success and happiness in terms of possessions and getting to do what he pleases. At this age, children don't hold grudges long, and you can rest easy knowing your relationship with your child will not be destroyed by garden-variety parent-child disputes.

Be firm, but understanding. The best way to help your tween cope with your refusal is to express it in terms of your beliefs and values rather than discipline and disapproval. If your child feels like he's being punished or that you're scornful of his desires, he may feel put down and become defiant. It's possible to show your child you understand his feelings while still saying no: "I know you're worried you'll be left out, and you want this really badly, but your friends will soon be into something else and they'll forget. Trust me." Or, "Every family's different. I believe our way is right for us, and I don't want to change it simply because your friend's family does it another way. Just tell him your parents won't let you."

Remain in charge, yet flexible. Chances are, there will be times when you concede on what feels like a string of things. When this happens, it can be helpful to use even an unimportant issue as an opportunity to stand your ground. You want to retain some authority with your child at this age, as he's still young. On the other hand, the answer shouldn't always be "no." Sometimes, merely stating your concerns can be enough to make your child aware of where you stand: "You can see I'm not happy about this, but because it's important to you, I'm going to allow you to do it."

Don't sweat the small stuff. When it comes to music, tweens typically like to explore and experiment—and to shock. It's usually not worth fretting or fighting over. Next week, they'll probably like something different, anyway. Rather than "Don't you dare listen to that stuff in this house," opt for the less confrontational—and judgmental—"Better you than me!"

EIGHT

Peer Pressure Can Be Used Positively to Change Behavior

Vladas Griskevicius, Robert B. Cialdini, and Noah J. Goldstein

> Vladas Griskevicius is a doctoral student in psychology at Arizona State University. Robert B. Cialdini is a Regents' Professor of Psychology and Marketing at Arizona State University. Noah J. Goldstein is an assistant professor of behavioral science at the University of Chicago Graduate School of Business. In the following viewpoint, they discuss how the general public is turning to the opinions of their friends and peers to determine what they will buy, how much they will drink, and other choices in life. Rather than succumbing to advertising to see a brand's appeal, people will buy what their friends buy. Moreover, the authors say, during periods of uncertainty, such as company mergers or management changes in their office, people will follow their peers even more closely in order to relate to others with shared experiences. Consequently, management should use a peer employee to explain a new policy, rather than a supervisor.

If everyone else jumped off a cliff, would you do it, too? In many ways, it's a ridiculous question. People don't follow one another, lemming-like, off cliffs. Moreover, although teenagers

Vladas Griskevicius, Robert B. Cialdini, and Noah J. Goldstein, "Applying (and Resisting) Peer Influence," *MITSloan Management Review*, vol. 49, Winter 2008, pp. 84–88. Copyright © Massachusetts Institute of Technology, 2008. All rights reserved. Reproduced by permission.

may be notorious for mimicking whatever their peers seem to be saying, doing or wearing, intelligent adults don't do something simply because others are. Or do they?

Scholars of various kinds have long documented the degree to which people are influenced by similar others, and social commentators have recently registered this phenomenon as well. For instance, *Time* magazine recently bestowed its coveted "Person of the Year" designation on an unsuspecting winner—us! In defense of the selection, the *Time* editors chronicled the extent to which consumers are abandoning traditional expert sources in favor of the perspectives of their peers. And because of the vast reach of the Internet, the range of "one anothers" now available is unprecedented. As a consequence, bloggers have become fonts of political wisdom; user groups dispense insights on everything from tea to technology; scholarship is entrusted to next-door-neighbor *Wikipedia* contributors; book sales are heavily influenced by Amazon.com customers' reviews; and the dominant restaurant guide in the United States—the *Zagat Survey*—recruits its raters exclusively from the ranks of nonprofessional critics.

Given all that, it's surprising how little business executives take note of the potency of peer influence at two crucial (and often-encountered) times: when, as tacticians, they seek to influence the actions of others, and when, as observers, they attempt to interpret the causes of their own actions. A close examination of these two failings reveals a number of ways in which they hamper effective managerial decision-making.

Influencing the Actions of Others

Savvy managers are aware of how people can be affected by the actions of similar others, but even they can fail to appreciate the full power of peer influence or to anticipate its unintended consequences. Such mistakes can be costly. Consider the Petrified Forest National Park in Arizona, which loses more than a ton of petrified wood each month because of theft. In hopes of preventing the vandalism, the park has instituted a deterrence program in which prominently placed signs make visitors aware of past thievery: "Your heritage is being vandalized every day by theft losses of petrified wood of 14 tons a year, mostly a small piece at a time."

Obviously, park officials want to deter potential offenders by describing the dismaying size of the problem, but an understanding of the inner workings of peer influence suggests that such a message might have undesirable unintended consequences. When one of our former graduate students visited the park with his fiancée—a woman he described as someone who would never take even a paperclip or rubber band without returning it—he was astonished when, after reading the sign decrying vandalism, she whispered to him, "We'd better get ours now."

What could have spurred that law-abiding woman to thievery and to think little of depleting a national treasure? The answer has to do with a mistake that park officials made when creating the sign. They tried to alert people to the problem by informing them of the scale of the losses. But in doing so, they inadvertently triggered the precise behavior they had hoped to suppress because they made thievery appear commonplace—when, in fact, only 2% of the park's millions of visitors have ever taken a piece of wood.

Look at All the People Who Are Doing It

The park officials are far from alone in their effort. Managers responsible for shaping or enforcing policy within an organization make similar blunders all the time. Because they don't give sufficient weight to the power of peer influence, they will frequently call attention to a problem behavior, such as supply room theft, by depicting it as regrettably frequent. Although such admonitions might be well-intentioned, the communicators have missed something critically important: Within the lament "Look at all the people who are doing this undesirable thing" lurks the powerful and undercutting disclosure "Look at all the people who *are* doing it." And in trying to alert people to the growing occurrence of a problem—which could be anything from expense account padding to safety violations—managers can inadvertently make it worse. Consider what occurred after the IRS [Internal Revenue Service] announced that it was going to strengthen the penalties for tax evasion because so many citizens were cheating on their returns. In the following year, tax fraud actually *increased*.

To explore how such messages can backfire, we conducted a test with our colleagues at the Petrified Forest. In the experiment, we used one of two signs in high-theft areas of the park. The first sign urged visitors not to take wood, and it depicted a scene showing several different thieves in action to highlight the problematic prevalence of the behavior. The second sign also urged visitors not to take wood, but it depicted only a lone thief. The results were unequivocal: Visitors who passed the first type of sign (which, incidentally, displays the type of information contained in the actual signage at the Petrified Forest) were more than twice as likely to steal the precious wood as those who passed the second type of sign. Thus, by failing to take into account the effects of peer influence, park administrators were actually achieving the opposite of what they had intended. Similarly, managerial efforts to stop a problem by calling attention to its prevalence can not only be ineffective but markedly counterproductive.

Going Green with Peer Influence

Frequently, that same mistake—underestimating the power of peer influence—also prevents managers from using persuasion tactics that *can* be highly effective in changing people's behaviors. Consider, for instance, the trend of businesses to become more environmentally conscious. Instead of highlighting how existing practices are harming the planet (not to mention a company's bottom line), shouldn't managers focus on what many employees have already been doing to preserve the environment, such as turning off lights and computers at the end of the day, recycling paper and so on?

To answer that question, we investigated the conservation efforts of hotels that display cards in rooms asking guests to reuse their towels. The cards can urge the action in various ways. Sometimes they request compliance for the sake of the environment;

other times they ask guests to conserve for the sake of future generations; and still other times they urge people to cooperate with the hotel in order to save water, energy and expense. But what the cards *never* say is that the majority of hotel guests do in fact reuse their towels when given the opportunity. We suspected that this omission was costing the hotels—and the environment—plenty.

So we tested that suspicion. In collaboration with the management of a major hotel in the Phoenix area, we put one of three different cards in the guestrooms. One card said HELP SAVE THE ENVIRONMENT; followed by information stressing the respect for nature. A different card stated PARTNER WITH US TO HELP SAVE THE ENVIRONMENT, followed by information urging guests to cooperate with the hotel in preserving the environment. A third card, using an appeal based on peer influence, said JOIN YOUR FELLOW GUESTS IN HELPING TO SAVE THE ENVIRONMENT, followed by information that the majority of hotel guests reuse their towels. The

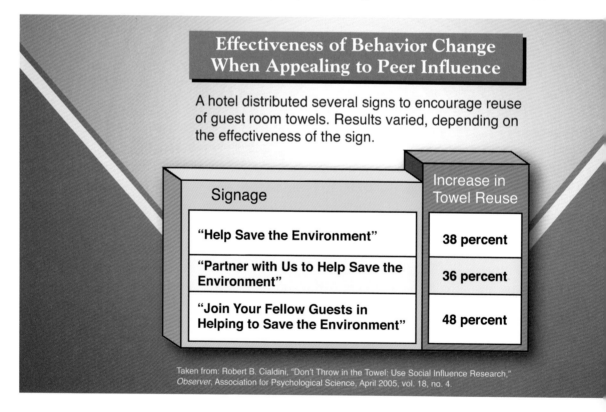

Effectiveness of Behavior Change When Appealing to Peer Influence

A hotel distributed several signs to encourage reuse of guest room towels. Results varied, depending on the effectiveness of the sign.

Signage	Increase in Towel Reuse
"Help Save the Environment"	38 percent
"Partner with Us to Help Save the Environment"	36 percent
"Join Your Fellow Guests in Helping to Save the Environment"	48 percent

Taken from: Robert B. Cialdini, "Don't Throw in the Towel: Use Social Influence Research," *Observer*, Association for Psychological Science, April 2005, vol. 18, no. 4.

outcome? Compared with the first two messages, the peer influence appeal resulted in a 34% increase in towel reuse.

The main lesson of the hotel experiment is that peer influence can be a powerful lever for change, but there's something else worth noting. The message that was the most successful in getting people to recycle their towels was one that, to our knowledge, no hotel has ever deployed. Apparently, the managers in charge of hotel conservation programs do not realize how effective a simple appeal based on peer influence can be.

Maximizing the Power of Peer Influence

By now, you've probably resolved never to make similar mistakes in your own efforts to persuade customers, clients, business prospects and coworkers. Good, but to maximize the effect of peer influence, consider this: The impact of peers increases during periods of uncertainty. Intuitively, this makes sense. After all, when people are unsure of what's happening around them, they don't look inside themselves for answers because all they'll see there is confusion. Instead, they look to the outside (that is, toward others) for clues about what to do. Thus, when business conditions have changed because of a merger, recent government regulation, a new competitor or some unforeseen economic event, employees will be especially attentive and responsive to information about how similar others are dealing with the unfamiliar conditions. That means that leaders will gain great persuasive leverage if they marshal and employ such information in their communications precisely at these times. All too often, though, managers rely on the wrong individuals to deliver important messages regarding impending change within the organization. That mistake can occur in one of two ways.

First, managers frequently take sole responsibility for communicating the wisdom of a new policy or initiative. But in doing so, they typically make the mistake of assigning too much power to their position in the organizational hierarchy or to their own persuasive abilities. In truth, the most effective communicators are those who know when they are *not* the best people to deliver a

Due to the power of positive peer influence, some experts say that news about workplace changes is best conveyed by employees to their peers, rather than by management.

message. More specifically, they recognize that, particularly during a period of uncertainty, the best route to influence others can be from the side rather than from above. For leaders, this means allowing employees who have yet to accept a change to hear from those who have, perhaps through team meetings. Even just one exposure to the favorable position of a peer can have a greater impact than multiple exposures to the similar position of a supervisor.

Second, when working to ensure that the voices of supportive employees will be heard, managers often select those who are the most articulate when they should instead favor those who are the most similar in circumstances to the individuals who are still unconvinced. So if resistance to an initiative is strongest among employees with the longest tenures, then a fellow old-timer who has genuinely embraced the change could be a better advocate than someone who might be more eloquent but has only recently come on board.

Buzz Marketing Increases Product Use

There's a related implication for marketers. When consumers have little or no experience with a brand or even with a general type of product or service, the resultant uncertainty will make them especially receptive to peer influence. That simple insight enabled one man to become a multimillionaire. His name was Sylvan Goldman and, after acquiring several small grocery stores in 1934, he noticed that his customers would stop buying items when their hand-held shopping baskets became too heavy. This led Goldman to develop the shopping cart. In its earliest form, the invention was a folding chair equipped with wheels and a pair of heavy metal baskets hanging off the sides. The contraption was so unfamiliar looking, though, that at first none of Goldman's customers was willing to use it, and their reluctance persisted even after he built an adequate supply, placed several of them in a prominent place in the store and erected signs describing the cart's use and benefits. Frustrated to the point of giving up, Goldman tried one more tactic: He hired shoppers to wheel the carts through the store while accumulating the items they wanted to purchase. As a result, his regular customers soon began following suit, and his invention swept the nation. Today, over three-quarters of a century later, the basic principle of Goldman's peer-based approach is the foundation of the increasingly popular form of word-of-mouth advertising called buzz marketing, in which companies employ highly visible consumers to use their new products and to create a "buzz" around them in the process. . . .

Making Better Decisions

We conducted an experiment at a busy subway station in New York City. In the test, we observed whether people chose to compensate a street musician by putting money in his hat. After getting a good measure of the percentage of passersby who gave to the performer, we changed the conditions slightly: Just before an approaching individual made a decision whether to make a contribution or not, we had another person (one of our colleagues) reach into his pocket and toss a few coins into the hat. The results were impressive: Passersby who saw someone make a donation were eight times more likely to contribute than those who didn't see anyone giving money.

But that wasn't the only noteworthy result. When the people who made a donation were interviewed, they all failed to attribute their action to the fact that they had seen someone else give money. Rather, they claimed that something else had been the cause—"I liked the song he was playing" or "I felt sorry for the guy" or "I had some extra change in my pocket." But because we had altered only one thing in the experiment—namely, the presence of a charitable individual—we knew that it wasn't any of those other factors that had made the difference. Instead, the key factor was the action of another person. Yet when our study's subjects thought about the reasons for their choices, not one of them hit upon the true cause. That finding illustrates a general psychological principle: People are often poor at recognizing why they behave as they do. The subway study also shows that people can be particularly clueless at recognizing that the actions of another person might be the cause of their own behavior.

Failure to Recognize Peer Influence

To probe that issue further, we conducted another experiment in which we and some colleagues arranged for residents of a midsize California community to receive appeals to conserve energy at home. The messages were printed on door hangers and were placed on the front door of each resident's house once a week for a month. The residents received one of four types of notes, emphasizing that energy conservation (1) helps the environment, (2) benefits society, (3) saves them money or (4) is common in their neighborhood—that is, the peer influence appeal. Subsequent interviews with household residents revealed that those who received the peer influence appeal rated it as the least likely to motivate them to conserve energy. Yet when we examined the actual energy usage of the community by recording electricity meter readings, we found that the peer influence appeal was the most effective, resulting in significantly greater energy conservation than any of the other messages.

The lesson from such studies is clear: When it comes to estimating the causes of their own conduct, people seem especially blind to the large role of peer influence. They don't just fail to get this right; they frequently get it precisely wrong. Consequently, managers need to recognize the stealthy impact that others' decisions can have on their own choices. When gathering information about the wisdom of a new initiative, for example, executives often collect data about the similar undertakings of decision makers in other units, organizations or industries. Because of the unrecognized power that such evidence will likely have, it is imperative that the data be culled only from those entities whose business circumstances and challenges are comparable to the situation at hand. . . .

Unethical Peer Influence

As with any technique for persuading others, peer influence can be used in unethical ways. Some individuals might be tempted to sway people by misinforming them about the beliefs, preferences or behaviors of "folks just like you." Consider the recent tactics of John Mackey, CEO [chief executive officer] of the Whole Foods Market Inc. grocery chain. In addition to hosting a blog on his company's Web site, Mackey regularly posted comments in Yahoo chat rooms to pump up his company's stock and degrade that of his main rival, all the while using an alias and proclaiming himself to be just another interested investor. The ethics of such behavior aside, that kind of covert misdirection—once brought to light—is likely to entail long-term costs for both the individuals using it and the companies that employ them.

Fortunately, peer influence can also be utilized in many ethical ways. A hotel, for example, doesn't need to resort to underhanded means to increase its towel reuse rate; it just needs to make guests aware that others are reusing their towels during their stay. Yet, as we've noted, that simple but effective measure has yet to be deployed. In sum, the opinions, experiences and behaviors of people's friends, neighbors and coworkers can provide an invaluable goldmine of persuasive resources. And that mine is, well, a terrible thing to waste.

NINE

Individuality Helps Girls Resist Peer Pressure

Beth Morrissey

Beth Morrissey, a librarian, writer, and researcher based in Dublin, Ireland, has published more than six hundred articles covering children's issues, women's issues, and parenting. In the following viewpoint she offers teenage girls some advice on how to resist peer pressure and do their own thing. Morrissey says it is OK to listen to your own music, babysit your siblings, be smart and do well in school, go shopping with your mom, participate in sports, and hang out with the unpopular kids.

Sure, it's great to fit in. But doing your own thing can be just as cool—and fun. Here's why. . . .

From making the cheerleading squad to scoring an invite to the party of the year, it's an awesome feeling to know you fit in. But if you're too intent on being part of the herd, it's easy to lose touch with your true identity—and all of the things that make you you. Like the soap opera says, you've only got one life to live. Why spend it stressin' about what others think? Go ahead and do your own thing whenever you want because. . .

It's OK . . . to groove to your own beat.
There's only so much Jonas Brothers that a girl can listen to without getting cavities. So if you feel like you need some real riffs in

Beth Morrissey, "Be the True You!" *Girls' Life*, vol. 14, August/September 2008, pp. 70–71. Reproduced by permission.

your life, hop online and dig up some underground sounds (music sites like iTunes often let you sample 30 seconds of music, which is a great way to explore new bands). Or, rifle through your mom's old CD collection for some classics—we bet you'll love Bruce Springsteen as much as she does. Musical tastes are very personal, so whatever gets you grooving is a good thing, even if it means no one will want to share your iPod again. Especially if it means no one will want to share your iPod again.

It's OK . . . to show off your smarts.
That big ol' brain of yours is stored with all sorts of info. So why keep all of that knowledge to yourself? Be proud to share your smarts in class: Impress your class with your fierce French accent,

"Black is unique, Mom. All the girls in school wear it."

wow 'em with your powerful poetry and raise your hand to answer Teach's tricky chem Q. As long as you're not a super show-off about your straight-A attitude, there's no need to keep your skills under wraps.

It's OK . . . to stay home with your little brother.
Your bro burps every five seconds and annoys you beyond belief. But once in a while, hanging with him instead of your friends on a Friday night can have its advantages. Not only will chilling with him score major points with the 'rents (hello, extended curfew!), but he can be tons of fun. After all, who else will challenge you to a foosball tournament (loser gets trash duty for a month!)? Or drink up a crazy concoction made of every liquid in the fridge just 'cause you dared him to? Never feel bad about passing on yet another aimless mall crawl—eventually your brother will be too big to boss around.

It's OK . . . to go to your dad for homework help.
Numbers are sooo not your strong suit. But Dad's a human calculator—and has a lot to offer when you need a little assistance with those algorithms. Having your dad as a tutor means he'll always be around when you need to cram before a big test, and there's no need to change out of your pajamas for a Sunday morning study session. And as Pops helps you pull up your grades, you can tutor him—starting with a fashion lesson (um, sorry, Dad, but black dress socks and Crocs just don't mix). Success all around!

It's OK . . . to like shopping with your mom.
Sure, most of your friends would rather die than go to Forever 21 with their moms. But you kinda dig Mom's honest feedback and practical approach to shopping (she was so right about you not needing those shiny pink leggings last spring!). It may be annoying when her fashion sense is more fashion nonsense, but if you've been able to get out of eating Brussels sprouts all these years, you can certainly sweet talk your way towards some cuter looks. Besides, sometimes shopping+mom=the clothes are on her.

There are benefits for teen girls who ignore peer pressure by shopping for clothes with their mothers.

It's OK . . . to fall for the geek.
Captain of the football team? Yawn. Student-council president? Maybe if you want to impress your grandmother. Captain of the Mathletes? Now we're talking! If you're more drawn to the soft-spoken smarty in your computer class than the current cutie-of-the-week, we don't blame you. After all, he does have some gorgeous eyes underneath those glasses, and he's as sweet as he is smart. So let your friends fight over the hottie du jour, you go after that geek!

It's OK . . . to follow the rules.
We'll admit: It's fun to break the rules on occasion. (Bacon and eggs for dinner? Why not!) But sometimes it's easier to stand by 'em—especially when that means you've got a built-in excuse to get out of stuff you know isn't a good idea. Like when your BFF

begs you to blow off band practice (when you really need to nail that new solo). No need to make up excuses for why you can't—just blame it on the rules. See? Life's easier already.

It's OK . . . to chill by yourself.
Remember "quiet time"? You probably hated it as a kid. But these days, your go, go, go schedule means that having an hour to chill alone can be pure bliss. When you're feeling stressed or are just in need of a break, recharge with some low-key "me" activities. Take a bubble bath. Paint your toenails. Reread your entire *Girls' Life* collection. Whatever you do, just be sure you're looking out for numero uno (that's you, silly).

It's OK . . . to rock your own style.
You know that sweet vest you found in your grandfather's closet that you've been afraid to wear because your BFF called it weird? Well, no offense to your girl, but who made her chief of the fashion police? Your personal style should be reflective of who you are, not what all of your friends are wearing. If your inner fashionista is urging you to rock that vest—or any other out-there item in your closet—go for it. The most important thing is to dress to impress yourself, so if you let what others think affect something as insignificant as your clothing choices, what does that say about your ability to stand up for yourself? If anyone questions your funky flair, who cares? Just tell 'em Rodrigo says it's the hottest style this year. (Don't worry. We don't know who he is, so they won't either.)

It's OK . . . to let loose on the field.
Feeling sporty? Then lace up your sneaks and hit the turf. Don't worry about your butt looking big in your uniform or the fact that Hottie McHighSchool might see you sweat as you run laps. Who knows, maybe Hottie has a thing for sporty girls who handle a field hockey stick with style. Or maybe you'll be so stoked by scoring the game-winning goal that you won't really care anyway. So what are you waiting for? Being a player isn't always a bad thing.

Peer Pressure to Use Drugs and Alcohol Can Be Combated

Do It Now Foundation

> Do It Now Foundation publishes and distributes pamphlets, booklets, posters, and educational materials to inform and guide children and adolescents through issues such as drugs and alcohol, sex, and family communication. In its pamphlet on peer pressure, reprinted here, the foundation discusses the role of peer pressure in teens' decisions about drugs and alcohol use. Everyone wants to feel cool and do what the cool kids are doing. But doing drugs and getting drunk have consequences, such as getting arrested, having a hangover, and altering brain chemistry.

We're decision-making animals, every one of us. From the moment we wake up and decide what kind of mood we're in to the final choice we make whether or not to floss our teeth at night, we're all making decisions, all the time.

We decide whether to shoot hoops or watch TV after school (or watch hoops on TV), and whether to have vanilla, chocolate, or Strawberry-Pickle Parfait at the local 57 Flavors.

On the other hand—or foot (we decided to be different), we also make a lot of decisions that don't even seem like decisions.

Jennifer James, "Peer Pressure & Choices: How to Think for Yourself (in a World Where Everybody Wants to Do It for You)," *FactsFirst!* 2004, pp. 1–2. Reproduced by permission of Do It Now Foundation.

Teens Are More Likely to Smoke If They Have Friends Who Smoke

A survey of twenty thousand teenagers in the United States led by Elizabeth Lloyd-Richardson of Brown University in Providence, Rhode Island, found:

- Teens who had at least two friends who smoked were more than six times as likely to become intermittent smokers than those whose friends didn't smoke.

- These teens were also ten times more likely than others to go from intermittent smoking to daily smoking.

- Teens who were alienated from their school environment were ten times more likely to start smoking than those who felt comfortable in school.

- Teenage boys were not influenced at all by their parents who smoked, while teenage girls whose mothers smoked were 36 percent more likely to start smoking.

Taken from: CBC News, "Peer Pressure Biggest Influence on Teen Smokers: Study," August 12, 2002.

Example: Passing when mom tries to pawn off turnips as food. That isn't a decision we spend a lot of time thinking about. Most of us just pass the bowl as fast as we can.

Saying "yes" or "no" (or "uh-huh" or "huh-huh") on the spur of the moment works pretty well most of the time. But big decisions need a little more attention. And choosing about drugs and alcohol is as big as decisions ever get.

That's what this pamphlet is all about.

In it, we'll discuss how to figure out what's right for you in making choices about drugs and alcohol.

We'll also talk about peer pressure and discuss how you can say "no"—if and when you need to—in a way that gets heard and respected.

That way, you won't have to be someone who says "yes" when you mean "no," and spend the rest of your life in therapy, wondering why no one understands you and waiting for your 50-minute "hour" of therapy to be up.

Sound worthwhile? You decide.

Peers and Pressures

The first thing we'll talk about is why people use drugs and alcohol in the first place.

There are as many different answers to that question as there are burgers at McDonald's: about 16 bazillion—and still counting.

Some people drink or do drugs to relax or forget their problems or have fun or fall asleep.

Others do it because they think everybody else does—and they're afraid they'll look clueless or totally out of it if they don't.

But if you peel away the first 16 bazillion layers of the onion, you'll find that most people get into drugs or drinking in the first place because someone they know is into it.

The fancy word for the process is peer pressure. It means that we feel pressure (either from inside or outside ourselves) to be like other people.

Peer pressure isn't a bad thing. It plays a big role in determining who we are and how we dress and talk and act.

It's a main reason that kids in America dress and talk and act more or less alike, instead of looking and acting and talking like people in Lithuania or Katmandu.

Still, peer pressure can cause problems, too. Because, sometimes, people in groups act differently and do things they'd never do on their own.

Why? Because we all lose at least some of our identity in a group. And the normal controls we put on our behavior can crumble before the need we all feel to fit in and be respected by others.

Peer pressure isn't always (or even usually) the obvious stuff they show in TV commercials. ("Wanna try a joint? No? Wussamadda? Chicken?")

More often, it's hard to even notice, much less resist.

But if you want to pull your own strings in life, you need to be aware of it and know how it works and learn how to make choices for yourself, in spite of it.

Truth or Consequences

Ever wonder why our society makes such a big deal out of drugs and alcohol—and spends so much time and money to talk you out of trying them?

It's not that drugs and alcohol are bad and ducking them is good, although a lot of people believe that.

Drugs are drugs. Period. Alcohol is alcohol. They're not good or bad. They're chemicals.

Think of if this way: Drugs and alcohol are like dynamite—it's not good or bad, either.

Use a couple of sticks to clear away a boulder that's blocking a road to a jungle hospital, and it's good. Use it to blow up the hospital, and it's bad.

Drugs are like that. Some have real value, but any chemical that can change the way you think and feel is something you need to consider carefully.

That's especially true because the effects of drugs and alcohol aren't external (like dyeing your hair green on St. Patrick's Day), but internal, and can cause real changes in the body and brain.

And even though some drug effects feel cool for a while (or people wouldn't do them), they always wear off.

Then the body-and-brain's owner is back at Square One, dealing with the consequences.

What consequences?

The same kind of stuff that follows in the wake of every choice we make. (If you choose chocolate, you can't have vanilla. Choose vanilla, and you can't have Strawberry-Pickle Parfait. Duh!)

Drugs and alcohol have consequences, too and some of them aren't cool, at all.

And it isn't just hangovers or failing in school or getting arrested that you need to consider—although those are real consequences that can affect the quality of your life for a long time.

There are other consequences, too, and we're just beginning to understand some of them—like the changes in brain chemistry that can follow periods of drug use.

Because the fact is that all drugs change brain chemistry somehow—or they wouldn't work at all.

And anything that powerful really ought to be treated with respect and taken a lot more seriously than some people take the choice to drink or do drugs.

A, B, or C—Made E-Z

Okay. So the downside of drugs has nothing to do with good or bad and everything to do with how they affect the quality of life—and the consequences they tend to leave behind.

That's why it's smart to think about drinking and drugs before you start bumping up against hard choices in the real world.

Because you know what happens if you put off thinking about important stuff.

It keeps on being important and you get more likely to do some dumb, spur-of-the-moment thing (especially if your friends are doing it), than what's best for you.

But how do you decide what you really want?

Try considering your options at each of the five stages that go into every decision.

Usually, we choose so fast that we don't realize just how detailed the process is.

But when you think about it, there really are five parts to every decision:

- **Identify** the problem (Turnips! Yipes!)
- **Describe** possible solutions or alternatives (Feed 'em to the dog! Spit 'em out! Close your eyes and swallow. . . .)
- **Evaluate** the ideas (The dog's outside! The napkin's too small! Just get it over with. . . .)
- **Act** out a plan (Play dead! Barf. . . .)
- **Learn** for the future (Find out beforehand what's for dinner and play sick if necessary. . . .)

Didn't know you were that complicated, huh?

In case you didn't notice, the first letter of each step spells out "IDEAL," and it is pretty much an ideal way to figure out what your options are in any situation—and predict possible consequences.

Yo, more turnips, anyone?

"I'm fine."

Often, a young teen's greatest challenge is not to succumb to peer pressure to experiment with drugs and alcohol.

Ways to Say No

Think things through, and if you come up with 16 bazillion and one reasons for not trying drugs and alcohol, remember that there are almost that many ways to say "no," should the need ever arise. You can say:

"Not tonight. I have to study."

"No, thanks. I'm in training."

"Nope, not for me!"

"Hey! No way!"

"Thanks, but no thanks." or

"Just leave me alone." Period.

But of all the ways anyone ever devised for saying "no" to drugs and alcohol, we like one better than all the rest.

We'll share it with you, in case you ever want to try it out yourself.

Just say: "I'm fine."

You really are, you know. You always have been.

The trick is keeping yourself that way. But you're up to it, aren't you?

One reason that way too many kids drink and do drugs is that they're afraid they'll look clueless or totally out of it, if they don't. Cool, huh?

ELEVEN

A Teacher Teaches Students About Peer Pressure

Jane Wingle

Jane Wingle teaches religion, English, and literature at St. Catherine of Siena School in Albany, New York. In the following viewpoint, she recounts an incident in her sixth-grade classroom in which one student decided to break the rules and stand rather than sit during a morning prayer. All but one other student followed the first student's lead. Wingle told her class that the first student who stood and the last student who refused to stand and remained seated were both leaders. The rest of the students were followers.

I teach religion first thing in the morning to 26 bright, creative sixth graders. Part of our morning ritual is to say prayer petitions. My students seem to be calmed by their expressions of care for their families, friends, pets, our military troops, victims of natural disasters, the homeless, etc. One morning this past spring, one student decided to shake things up a bit. . . .

My students and I always remain seated for the petition part of prayer. It's a lengthy process and I've found that standing through it impedes the children's ability to concentrate. On this particular day, I asked one of the boys to begin with his petitions. He stood, with just a hint of a smirk on his face, said his petitions

Jane Wingle, "The Power of Peer Pressure," *Teaching K–8*, November/December 2006, pp. 50–51. Reproduced by permission of Highlights for Children Inc., Columbus, Ohio.

and remained standing. It's my practice to only interrupt the prayer process if absolutely necessary. I thought it was strange that he was standing, but ignored it and called on the next student. He noticed that his buddy was standing, grinned, prayed and remained standing. I thought it potentially troublesome but stuck to my policy and didn't interrupt. Then it got interesting. . . .

Students Make a Decision

The next student, a boy not inclined toward mischief, started his petitions sitting down. As he spoke, he looked at the other two boys who were still standing. In those brief seconds he blushed

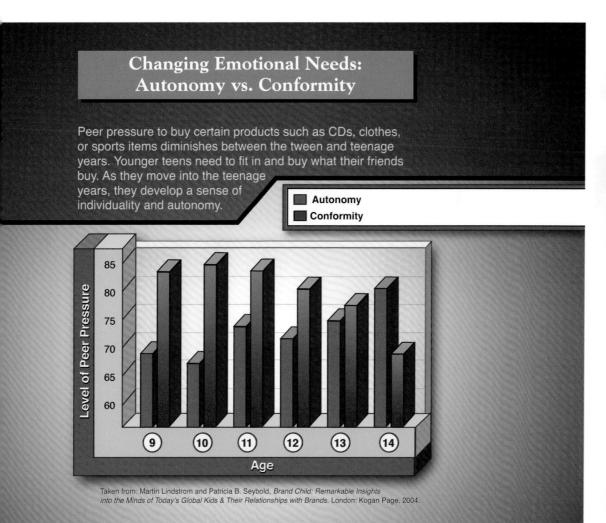

Taken from: Martin Lindstrom and Patricia B. Seybold, *Brand Child: Remarkable Insights into the Minds of Today's Global Kids & Their Relationships with Brands.* London: Kogan Page, 2004.

and looked very uncomfortable, but finally stood just as he finished his prayer. The other two remained silent. There was no badgering; they just stood. . . .

The next two students, both girls, remained seated during their petitions, but neither looked at ease. The next two stood without hesitation. The next, a boy, hesitated, but begrudgingly stood. It was at this time that I heard one of the seated girls mumble to herself in an exasperated tone, "Oh, I guess I better stand." Immediately, the next seated girl followed suit. The next 15 students stood, one right after the other, without hesitation. This group included one boy who hadn't said a single petition all year. On this morning, however, he said a list of petitions so he could stand and follow the crowd. Two students were absent. One of them entered during this process. He didn't even question what was happening. He just stood. Finally, we got to the last student, a girl, who said her petitions in a seated position and remained seated.

I stared at my class. Apparently, they saw the bemused look on my face because all but the one girl remained standing and stared right back at me. They did not giggle; they did not speak. This had obviously not been planned, and I don't believe any of the standing students, except possibly the one who started it, knew why they were standing. Finally, I said, "You have just demonstrated in the clearest way possible the power of peer pressure. I know some of you are natural leaders and some of you are more inclined to follow, but today, only two of you are leaders—the one who started this and the one who remained sitting." . . .

Leaders and Followers

Knowing sixth grade students, and seeing the pained and annoyed looks on many of their faces, I decided to pursue this issue later on an individual basis. I knew some students were a little embarrassed by what they had done. If I had pursued this matter through a class conversation, most would have tried to save face and I wouldn't have gotten to the heart of why so many, even the "born leaders," decided to be followers. I spent the next two days interviewing individuals for two or three minutes. All I asked was, "Why did you remain standing?" Here are some of the answers I received.

The boy who initiated the activity said, "I don't know. I just did." His buddy, who was second in the progression, said, "I did it because he did it." The third, the boy who hesitated, said, "I noticed that they were standing after I started talking, so I stood." The next boy I asked looked at the one who had started it (he happened to enter the room) and said, "Because I wanted to and because he did it and he's cool."

I asked the one brave soul why she didn't stand. Being last in line and a thinker, she had had time to assess the situation. She said, "I was watching everybody. My brain said, 'Don't stand. Be an individual.' I didn't want to be like everyone else." The last student questioned, a girl, said, "[I stood] because people would think I'd be ruining the plan and they would get mad at me." She didn't realize there was no plan. . . .

A Learning Experience

I decided that the next morning I would ask each student to write his or her answer to one more question. First, we discussed the situation a bit and the class seemed a little more at ease with what had happened. They are a smart and reactive group and seemed happy to respond, perhaps putting closure to this brief, yet meaningful event in their lives. I asked, "What did you learn?" Some of my student's insights were remarkable. . . .

Six students said they learned nothing and one of those added, "I didn't have to stand, but I wanted to." The majority of those six students, interestingly enough, show some leadership potential. It's my guess that a few were embarrassed about the fact that they had taken on the role of follower. Two other students responded that the only reason they stood was because they didn't realize their actions had anything to do with peer pressure. These are both relatively independent girls. Had they thought about what they were doing, they might not have followed. Here are some other perceptive responses:

Teachers can have a powerful impact on students by teaching them about leadership skills that enhance their ability to resist peer pressure.

- "I learned that I shouldn't do things just because other people do."
- "I learned that most kids will follow what a couple of kids start."
- "If a couple of kids follow one kid, the whole group might follow, even if they don't want to."
- "I learned that even if everyone is doing something, you don't have to follow, especially if it makes you uncomfortable."

- "I learned that peer pressure is a very powerful thing. It can cause you to do something that you may not want to do. It can be dangerous at times and make you act like a totally different person than you really are."
- "I have learned that peer pressure can be like a wildfire and spreads fast."

This was the kind of teachable moment that presents itself without an outline or lesson plan. My students taught me something that beautiful spring day. Watch what children do and take advantage of what they can learn from their own interactions: ultimately, they are their own best teachers.

TWELVE

A Girl Remembers a Boy Who Resisted Peer Pressure

Penny S. Harmon

Penny S. Harmon is a real estate agent in Maine and a travel writer. In the following viewpoint she recounts an incident during her seventh-grade year when a boy, Danny, stood up for himself and was not afraid of what his classmates thought of him. Although poor, Danny stood up and told his teacher that he would not ask his parents for money for a class trip. Penny, who was also poor, had always hidden her family's economic status, embarrassed that her friends would think less of her. After Danny's pronouncement, she admired him for his courage and refusal to bow to peer pressure. She no longer felt she had to lie to others or to find excuses for why she could not afford to do things with her friends.

Patterning your life around other's opinions is nothing more than slavery.

Lawana Blackwell

I was in seventh grade when Danny transferred to my school and became my first real crush. He had the darkest of brown eyes and light blond hair with a dark complexion. I fell for

Danny the first day he arrived, and many of the girls in my class felt the same way. That, however, soon changed.

Danny had been going to our school for about a week when his parents picked him up in an old beat-up car that spewed exhaust and made loud banging sounds. The girls who had previously adored him looked disgusted. It was obvious that Danny was poor and that was that. He was no longer boyfriend material.

I had a poor family as well; I just hid it from everyone. I was so ashamed of how we lived that I never had kids come over to my house. Even though I couldn't do a thing about it, I felt like the kids in my class would judge me if they knew the truth. It was a lot of work keeping my secret, but I figured it was easier than it would be to not have any friends.

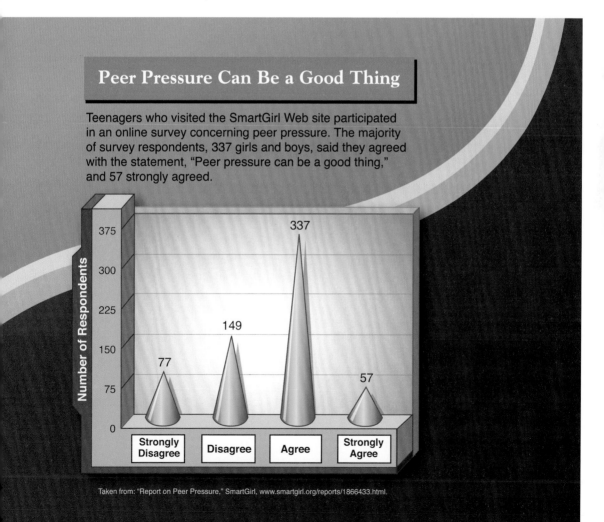

Peer Pressure Can Be a Good Thing

Teenagers who visited the SmartGirl Web site participated in an online survey concerning peer pressure. The majority of survey respondents, 337 girls and boys, said they agreed with the statement, "Peer pressure can be a good thing," and 57 strongly agreed.

Number of Respondents

375
300
225
150
75
0

337
149
77
57

Strongly Disagree | Disagree | Agree | Strongly Agree

Do Not Hide the Truth

One day, our teacher, Mr. Sims, announced that the seventh-grade field trip would be to an amusement park. The classroom buzzed with excitement as the girls discussed what they would wear and what they should bring with them. I sat back and listened, knowing that my parents did not have the money to send me. It made me angry to feel so left out. But not Danny. He simply told everyone that he wouldn't be going. When Mr. Sims asked him why, Danny stood up and stated, "It's too much money right now. My dad hurt his back and has been out of work for a while. I'm not asking my parents for money."

Sitting back down in his seat, Danny held his head up proudly, even though whispering had begun. I could only shrink in my seat, knowing those whispers could be about me when they found out I would not be going either.

"Dan, I'm very proud of you for understanding the situation that your parents are in. Not every student your age has that capability," he replied.

Glaring at the students whispering in the back, Mr. Sims spoke again, only louder.

"This year, we're going to do things differently. The trip is not until the end of the month, so we have plenty of time for fund-raising. Each student will be responsible for bringing in at least one idea for a fund-raising drive. Bring them in tomorrow. If a student does not want to contribute to the drive, then he or she will be spending the field trip day here at the school. Any questions?"

Of course, Shelly, the most popular girl in the class, spoke up.

"Well, Mr. Sims, my parents can afford it. Do I still have to help?"

"Shelly, this is not a matter of being able to afford it. Money is not just something that is handed to you when you get older. This will be a great learning experience for everyone, whether you have the money or not."

Be Accepted for Who You Are

While walking home from school that day, I noticed three of the boys from our class talking with Danny. I worried that they were

It takes courage for a young person to stand up to peer pressure but, by doing so, he or she can influence others to do the same.

giving him a hard time, but as I got closer, I realized they weren't harassing him. They were all just debating about the best ideas for a fund-raiser.

Although not everyone accepted Danny after that day, he won over the respect of many of us. I was especially awed by how he didn't cave under peer pressure. For so long, I could never admit to my friends that I could not afford to go somewhere. Instead, in order to continue to fit in, I lied about why I couldn't do things and came up with excuse after excuse.

By standing up and admitting he was poor, Danny changed my life. His self-confidence made it easier for all of us to understand that what his parents had or didn't have did not determine who he was. After that, I no longer felt I had to lie about my family's situation. And the funny thing was, those who were truly my friends stuck by me when I finally let them get closer.

And Danny, more because of his courage and honesty than his great looks, is someone I will never forget.

What You Should Know About Peer Pressure

What Peer Pressure Is
- Following the crowd, doing whatever everyone else is doing.
- Allowing others to talk you into doing something that you feel uncomfortable doing or is against the law.
- Not wanting to feel left out or weird or alone.
- Fearing the loss of friends if you do not do what they want.
- Believing it is more important to fit in than it is to follow the rules or do what is right.

Facts About Peer Pressure
- In a study by the Kaiser Family Foundation, 33 percent of boys ages fifteen to seventeen and 23 percent of girls reported feeling peer pressure to have sex.
- SADD (Students Against Destructive Decisions) reports that 30 percent of high school students who have a good relationship with their parents have used drugs, while 48 percent who have a weak relationship with their parents have used drugs.
- Negative peer pressure disproportionately affects minorities in academic performance. In a National Assessment of Education Progress study, 36 percent of fourth-grade black students, 29 percent of Hispanic students, and only 17 percent

of white students reported that their friends made fun of them for getting good grades in school.

• Peer pressure is strongest in tweens (ages eight to twelve) than in later adolescence.

• Adolescents may have a predisposition toward peer pressure. Brain researchers are finding that adolescents do not yet have the impulse control necessary to make the rational decisions that adults are capable of.

• Not all peer pressure is bad. Positive peer pressure can encourage teens to be a good team member, volunteer for projects, and not engage in risky behavior.

• Peer pressure affects people of all ages, not just children or teens.

• Adults feel peer pressure at work, to make them do a good job or to behave ethically, or in their community, to participate in environmental cleanup events or parent/student programs.

What You Should Do About Peer Pressure

Confront Peer Pressure

Young people have many weapons against peer pressure. It may not always be easy to say no to the crowd, walk away when people are doing something you think is wrong, listen to different music, or hang out with the unpopular kids. Peer pressure loses its power when the many generally good kids refuse to follow the few aggressive or destructive kids. Reverse peer pressure works when the few leaders of the gang do not want to be the only kids vandalizing, smoking, or drinking when they see that no one else is doing it with them.

Kids who want to resist peer pressure can talk to a parent, teacher, coach, or school nurse if they feel they are being pressured into doing something they do not want to do or are not ready for. They can also directly confront the kids who are pressuring them by making eye contact, standing up straight, and simply stating that they do not want to follow along, then walking away. Various phrases kids can use include an outright "No," or, "Maybe later," "I don't think I should do that," or, "My parents will ground me."

Avoid Peer Pressure

Kids who resist peer pressure might get teased for not going along with the crowd, but they might also gain some respect among other kids for standing their ground and sticking up for their own principles. They might also make some new friends who admire their courage to do their own thing.

One scientifically proven way to avoid destructive peer pressure is to get involved in sports. Participating in sports boosts a person's self-esteem, sense of achievement, decision-making ability, and cooperation skills. Teens who are part of a sports team learn to work together and to create a sense of achievement.

Parents Can Help Teens Resist Peer Pressure

Parents have a role to play as well. Parents should remain vigilant in monitoring their teens' behavior to make sure they are not breaking the law or participating in harmful or risky activities. But parents should not be too stifling or strict in matters that are not such a big deal, such as what music their kids listen to, what clothes their kids wear, or who their kids socialize with. These choices help young people build self-esteem and develop decision-making skills.

Parents have more influence over their kids than they think they do. Young people appreciate adults taking an interest in their likes and dislikes, being concerned about their safety, and protecting them from drugs, sex, or smoking. Many kids say their mom or dad is the person they admire and respect most. Parents should take advantage of this. By creating role-playing scenarios to help their children avoid peer pressure and develop self-esteem, parents let them know they have a safe place to turn if they get into trouble.

ORGANIZATIONS TO CONTACT

The editors have compiled the following list of organizations concerned with the issues debated in this book. The descriptions are derived from materials provided by the organizations. All have publications or information available for interested readers. The list was compiled on the date of publication of the present volume; the information provided here may change. Be aware that many organizations take several weeks or longer to respond to inquiries, so allow as much time as possible.

Advocates for Youth
2000 M St. NW, Ste. 750, Washington, DC 20036
(202) 419-3420
Web site: www.advocatesforyouth.org

Advocates for Youth creates programs and advocates for policies that help young people make responsible decisions about their reproductive and sexual health. Its Web site offers a youth forum, information on youth activist campaigns, and tips on health and well-being. Its online publication *Issues at a Glance* offers information on peer education, promoting healthy behavior, sexual health, prevention, and life skills.

Al-Anon/Alateen
1600 Corporate Landing Pkwy., Virginia Beach, VA 23454-5617
(757) 563-1600
Web site: www.al-anon.alateen.org

A1-Anon and Alateen help families, friends, and relatives of alcoholics share their experiences to resolve their common problems. Al-Anon's monthly magazine, *The Forum*, contains inspirational stories, personal views, and experiences of members. Al-Anon's book, *The Dilemma of the Alcoholic Marriage*, covers the difficulty in being married to an alcoholic.

American Academy of Child and Adolescent Psychiatry (AACAP)
3615 Wisconsin Ave. NW, Washington, DC 20016-3007
(202) 966-7300
Web site: www.aacap.org

AACAP is composed of child and adolescent psychiatrists who actively research, evaluate, diagnose, and treat psychiatric disorders. The organization's publication *Facts for Families* provides current information on issues that affect children, teenagers, and their families, such as emotional situations, behavior problems, substance abuse, and peer pressure. The academy's Web site also offers books and journal articles on adolescent psychiatry topics.

Big Brothers/Big Sisters
230 N. Thirteenth St., Philadelphia, PA 19107
(215) 567-7000
Web site: www.bbbs.org

Big Brothers/Big Sisters is a youth mentoring organization that provides positive relationships for children that have a direct and measurable impact on their lives. In community-based mentoring, children and their mentors meet in their community to share activities, while in school-based mentoring, they meet at schools, libraries, and community centers. Big Brothers/Big Sisters also has a Hispanic program and one for children who have a parent in prison, called "Amachi."

Bureau for At-Risk Youth
PO Box 1246, Wilkes-Barre, PA 18703-1246
(800) 999-6884
Web site: www.at-risk.com

The Bureau for At-Risk Youth provides publications and prevention materials for grade schools, youth services, and juvenile justice organizations. The bureau's LifeSteps series of books for children in grades six through twelve offers dramatizations and problem-solving sessions to help students develop character, responsibility, empathy, and the courage to avoid alcohol and drugs and to make healthy choices during their lives.

Girls Circle Association

458 Christensen Ln., Cotati, CA 94932
(707) 794-9477
Web site: www.girlscircle.com

Girls Circle provides gender-specific programs for girls to provide social support, improve self-esteem and body image, and prevent risky behaviors. The *Girls Circle Facilitator Activity Guides* offer eight- to twelve-week programs that provide skill-building activities to promote girls' critical thinking and develop confidence, honesty, and communication skills. Topics include friendship, body image, relationships with peers, and expressing individuality.

Healthy Teen Network (HTN)

1501 Saint Paul St., Ste. 124, Baltimore, MD 21202
(410) 685-0410
Web site: www.healthyteennetwork.org

HTN is a national organization that provides information, training, advocacy, and programs in the areas of teen parents, teen pregnancy, and teen pregnancy prevention. HTN offers the *Opportunity Knocks* newsletter that provides information on abstaining from sex and using contraceptives, so teens can make responsible decisions. Its booklet *The Times They Are A Changin'* presents an open dialogue about diversity, and *Boys Will Be Boys* talks about gender-specific violence.

KidsHealth

Web site: http://kidshealth.org

Created by the Nemours Foundation's Center for Children's Health Media, KidsHealth provides doctor-approved health information for children, teens, and parents through in-depth features, articles, games, and resources. Its Web site provides quizzes, Q&A, facts, discussions, news, recipes, healthcare information, safety tips, fitness tips, mental health information, and more for teens to share.

Mothers Against Peer Pressure (MAPP)
2152 Ralph Ave., Ste. 707, Brooklyn, NY 11234
Web site: www.mothersagainstpeerpressure.org

MAPP is a nonprofit organization to help parents counteract peer pressure in their children's lives with information on GED (general equivalency diploma) resources and the dangers of prison, sexually transmitted diseases, and domestic violence. The organization offers Teen Challenge programs, which are residential and nonresidential programs for adolescents seeking freedom from life-controlling problems. The group also broadcasts and streams a weekly radio show.

Students Against Destructive Decisions (SADD)
SADD National
255 Main St., Marlborough, MA 01752
(877) 723-3462
Web site: www.sadd.org/

SADD (formerly Students Against Driving Drunk) provides prevention and intervention to young people in the areas of destructive decisions such as underage drinking, drug use, teen violence, and suicide. SADD's newsletter, *Decisions*, discusses such topics as prevention techniques, bringing families together, school safety, alcoholism, prom night responsibility, social networking sites, driving tips, and the dangers of inhalants. Its Web site also offers communication tips, statistics, and public service announcements.

Students Against Violence Everywhere (SAVE)
322 Chapanoke Rd., Ste. 110, Raleigh, NC 27603
(866) 343-7283
Web site: www.nationalsave.org

SAVE is a student-driven organization that helps young people learn about alternatives to violence through school and community service projects. Its Web site offers a forum in which students can talk about starting a SAVE chapter in their school, cyberbullying, teen dating violence, school safety, substance abuse, gang violence, natural disaster recovery efforts, and relationships between students and teachers.

BIBLIOGRAPHY

Books

Carolyn B. Anderson, *Let's Talk About Peer Pressure*. Montgomery, AL: E-BookTime, 2007.

Jim Auer and R.W. Alley, *Standing Up to Peer Pressure: A Guide to Being True to You*. St. Meinrad, IN: Abbey, 2003.

Hilary Cherniss and Sara Jane Sluke, *The Complete Idiot's Guide to Surviving Peer Pressure for Teens*. New York: Alpha, 2001.

Al Desetta, ed., *The Courage to Be Yourself: True Stories by Teens About Cliques, Conflicts, and Overcoming Peer Pressure*. Minneapolis: Free Spirit, 2005.

Robyn M. Feller, *Everything You Need to Know About Peer Pressure*. New York: Rosen, 2001.

Sandray Humphrey, *Hot Issues, Cool Choices: Facing Bullies, Peer Pressure, Popularity, and Put-Downs*. Amherst, NY: Prometheus, 2008.

Mitchell J. Prinstein and Kenneth A. Dodge, ed., *Understanding Peer Influence in Children and Adolescents*. New York: Guilford, 2008.

Elaine Slavens and Ben Shannon, *Peer Pressure: Deal with It Without Losing Your Cool*. Toronto: Lorimer, 2004.

Chris Widener, *Art of Influence: Persuading Others Begins with You*. New York: Doubleday Business, 2008.

Youth Communication, *Keeping It Real: Teens Write About Peer Pressure*. New York: Youth Communication, 2005.

Periodicals

Ian Ayres and Barry Nalebuff, "Peer Pressure," *Forbes*, April 11, 2005.

Debra Bass, "Helping Your Teen Overcome Negative Peer Pressure," American Counseling Association, *Counseling Corner*, August 4, 2008.

Business Wire, "HealthAmerica KidsHealth Gives Parents Advice on Child's Peer Pressure; How to Respond to 'Everyone's Doing It,'" August 3, 2006.

Matt Garrett, "Parenting in the Face of Peer Pressure," *Parenting*, December 5, 2007.

Kendra Hurley, "The Power of Peer Pressure," *Youth Media Reporter*, March 21, 2005.

Elise Kramer, "Peer Pressure," *Psychology Today*, September/October 2004.

Jennifer Levitz, "Can Your Friends Make You Fat?" *Wall Street Journal*, July 26, 2007.

New York Times Upfront, "Teens and Decision Making: What Brain Science Reveals," April 14, 2008.

Virginia Postrel, "Inconspicuous Consumption," *Atlantic Monthly*, July/August 2008.

Sally Squires, "Peer Pressure Can Carry Great Weight in Girls' Eating and Exercise Habits," *Washington Post*, July 15, 2008.

Teen People, "Real Kids Ask Real Kids. Answer: Peer Pressure," May 2004.

Robert Teese and Graham Bradley, "Predicting Recklessness in Emerging Adults: A Test of a Psychosocial Model," *Journal of Social Psychology*, 2008.

Rachel Whitaker, "Battling the Pressure," *Winner*, December 2007.

INDEX